STANDING ON EARTH

Phoneme Media
P.O. Box 411272
Los Angeles, CA 90041

First Edition, 2016

ISBN: 978-1-944700-00-3

This book is distributed by Publishers Group West

Cover art by Mokarrameh Ghanbari
Cover design and typesetting by Jaya Nicely

Printed in the United States of America

Phoneme Media is a nonprofit media company dedicated to promoting cross-cultural understanding, connecting people and ideas through translated books and films.

http://phoneme.media

Curious books for curious people.

STANDING ON EARTH

MOHSEN EMADI

TRANSLATED FROM THE PERSIAN BY LYN COFFIN

I was there.
An unborn child
playful among guns.
The sun rises
and I carry your death,
womb by womb.
Pomegranates trees start shaking
in my mother's nightmares.
One thousand moons fall from the branches.
A mirror breaks and in every broken piece
my mother gives birth.
In all the pieces,
I am crying and opening pomegranates with my thumbs.

What are you doing here? he asked.
I didn't know.
I woke up
in a song he wasn't singing.
The stars were in him,
lost lakes in me.
The moon was in him,
waxing and waning in me.
Lips were in him,
kissing in me.
Sparrows were sleeping on the vines of my veins,
what the bullets were saying startled them.
They kept hitting their heads on the edge of my body.
They flew away through my shadow.
In the rhythm of a shovel,
entering and leaving the earth,
a cradle was rocking far away and
my mother was emptying it

of sand.
Different deaths
eluded me.
With every new change of clothing
I wore a new death.
Your death
stole me from all of them.
It wanted to be mine.
Silence by silence
it turned to pomegranates in my mouth and
silence by silence
it fell like rain in my mother's lullaby and
silence by silence
I arrived where you are,
word by word,
poem by poem.

to Abbas Meftahi (1945-1972, executed by a firing squad)

Love Song

When the earthquake comes,
we and our words will camp in the fields.
In one day, the wheat will be ready to harvest
and the harvesters
will harvest us and our words
and set fire to the camps.
Then, the size of our coffin will be 8 by 10
and our names will be photocopied.

Tell the earthquake to come.

The city said,
Count me in.
It was your turn to hide.
If it were me
I would have chosen
the city's most crowded street,
with a lot of people
and the voice of a megaphone
and the siren of police cars.
But you remembered
windows in the alleys of your childhood.
You hid and no one ever found you.

No one remembers his birth.
No one has ever returned from the dead.
Words and death give meaning to everything.
Only meeting those surrounded by death
do words become proportionate.
You're standing there,
your back to the window.
A star flickers near your eyes.
Maybe the distance between us
is longer than the life of all words.
I come to bed with you
in the prehistory of words.
That star died centuries ago.
That light is just the last breath
traveling
through the void between stars,
through the void between words.
I kiss you
and I don't know
through what void,
what words,
what history
the flavor of this kiss has passed.

At sixteen
you wanted to be the skirt that embraced her nakedness
At twenty-five
you were a balloon in her hands
for her to burst
or a newspaper with the bold headline—"King Escapes!"
from which she made a paper hat
or she fired at you whenever she liked.
At sixty perhaps
you are the silence of a grave,
waiting to make love for centuries.
But at thirty
the distance between a skirt and the grave
is a poem.

I hang out my poem under the sun.
My sixteen years evaporate,
my twenty-five years burst,
my sixty years leak droplets.

And my thirty years
take the poem off the clothesline,
crumple it,
and all alone
walk away.

You look at me.
I recognize a thousand shadows of my self.
Short shadows, long shadows,
shadows that escape,
shadows that caress the hair of a woman,
shadows that grab the neck of a woman,
shadows that pass me,
shadows that get left behind,
and a shadow that covers your eyes with two hands
and whispers, *guess who,*
and a shadow that covers my eyes with two hands
and whispers, *and, now, guess who.*

A woman uses makeup
in her effort to be a Goddess.
No woman
uses makeup trying to be human.
She says: look at me,
pray to me.

In the solitude of all the goddesses,
she gives birth to the children.

Half mortal,
half immortal.
I always fail
to describe her artificial beauty
in my poetry.

As much as the poem does not need beauty,
she needs my kisses.

No woman
could make me naked,
could expose me or cover me up.

The voice I hear is coming from an imaginary corner.
Unseen hands open my shirt.
My skin trembles
and the cities built on it collapse
and my body disappears in a cloud of dust.

I close the curtains,
I unplug the phone,
I lie down on the floor
and people are fleeing in the dust cloud of my body,
in pyjama bottoms, in underpants, naked.

Cracks open in the ground of my skin.
Antique jars come to the surface,
the skeletons of women buried in me,
birthday presents, letters, photos.
The voice I hear enters the cracks in my skin.

But now the room's walls are moist.
Now the roof is leaking.
Now the doorbell is wet.
I open the door
and the stairs are flooded.

Your shoes, your voice, are soaking.
You open the windows.
You sweep up the fragments of words.
Kiss by kiss,

you stitch together the cracks in my body
You wrap me up.
I hear your voice rising from a dark corner.
I do not shake
in your embrace.

It's night.
You've left the house.
Stars are dust.
Nakedness is dust.
Every night
my room
goes dark,
gets light.

I write
where a word is an absence,
the mouth of a grave
leading directly to the belly of nothingness.
I write
where language is a funeral,
where the ritual of syntax
drowns in a hole
leading directly to the hunger of existence,
to nothingness.
I write
where subjective pronouns are massacres,
where all women die in you,
all children die in him,
and everyone dies in me.
I write
where to write is to drink poison,
and death
is a song,
whose music makes existence possible.

They're returning
from the burial.
Everyone has carried off his memories of the house—
the door, the window,
the window frame, curtains, carpets,
the heater, the stove, crockery...
The house is left without a door handle or a fire:
everyone has carried off his share of memories—
the opening and closing of the first door
the first waiting, the first fire

I climb the stairs of myself.
Cats run away.
It's cold.
I sit on a gate that's gone.
Snakes twist their way through me

At dawn
I see myself in a shard of a shattered mirror,
without memory,
without a handle,
without a fire,
without myself.

When nobody is supposed to come
you prepare your house for your fantasies.
It's not necessary to dye your white hair.
You walk around in your white undershirt
and stroke the long mane of a white horse
who has one bad leg.
You drag dead kittens out from under the sofas
and bury them under haystacks of white paper.
In the saddlebags of the horse
you find a sheet of music,
you sit at the piano of your sixteenth year.
All the notes are notes of farewell.
Farewells are floating in the air,
in the look of the horse,
in the perfume of all the people who died in your writing,
in the doorbell which is mute,
and the moon which moved out of the frames of your
windows.
In each farewell
a new fantasy comes to your house.
You prepare the house for it.

When you close your eyes
my mare rears up,
a panther lingers near the village,
and the jinns throw stones at each other.

Every night you look at me as if I'd killed a dictator,
as if I were a wanted man.
Sometimes you open your eyes
and you see me on vacation from jail,
or maybe resurrected from the grave.
But my mare is in her stall.
The panther is in my sight.
And the djinns are hidden in my pockets.

Outside it's raining and you're looking at me.
It is not clear why my mare bangs against the door,
neighing.
The panther claws my sight and I cry.
I put my hand in my pocket and there are no djinns there.
I bring out the metal coldness of a revolver
and I shoot at the rain.
The curtain of day falls.
You take your head in your hands and your heart beats
quickly.
Strangers pull the door off its hinges and take me with
them.
Drag me down the stairs, across the wet asphalt and
papers.
Somewhere in the middle of the words
the command —*Fire!* sets the paper burning.
Outside it's raining and you're looking at me.
As usual, I'm coming back from my grave.

One day the sea dies.
One day the earth dies.
We left the sea and the earth to the Gods .
We sat and thought of that day
we discovered love
and betrayal
and slowly
we forgot the Gods.

The sea brings the dead body of a girl to the shore.
We are whispering.
Perhaps love suits her,
perhaps betrayal....

The wave foam soft sand
swollen face dark lips.
With our whispers
we come to the cemetery.
The earth covers her face,
covers her lips,
covers her kisses.
We return to our house,
taking with us
only love
and betrayal?

We carry their weight with us everywhere:
photographs
in our wallets, in our pockets,
hung from our car mirrors,
in our bed frames.
Little by little they become part of us,
like our hair.
Today we cut them,
tomorrow they grow.
An itching in our bodies announces their presence.
They die a little after us.
Even when our coffin lid is closed,
for a few mornings, they continue to grow.

Covered with a white sheet,
surrounded by a circle of mourning phantoms,
with the weightless weight of a white rose on your chest.

Little by little
consciousness
evaporates
but the body
still feels an itch.
You get up
and look at that crumpled face
in the photo
and you cry.

It Is Snowing

I

It is snowing outside. I'm listening to a song. Twice in this song I've fallen in love. I don't know what language the song is in. It makes no difference because I dream in one language and I fall in love in another. Last year, I changed my residence five times. Last year, on the stairs in my building, I saw a dead bird. I was afraid to bury her. Maybe the woman who cleaned the building threw the bird away, but for a whole year, I have been burying her in different countries. This is absolute egoism on my part. Burying a dead bird doesn't affect the bird, it just saves me having to watch her decay. But why should I be afraid of decay? I, who lived through the longest war of the last century and who fell in love a few years after the dictator died, I who in later years preferred displacement to the next dictator. The fear of decay can't be the same as the fear of death. It also does not depend on location. It more closely resembles the fear of ugliness. Burial is a matter of aesthetics. But aesthetics just opens a discussion about the necessity or non-necessity of burying the bird and does not say anything about my fear. It doesn't mention I was afraid to touch the bird, even though I had touched several dead people. Some even died in my arms. Also sometimes I doubt whether I'm still alive. This is not strange for someone who falls asleep in one city and wakes up in another city. Perhaps I was afraid I would catch something if I touched the dead body of the bird. Maybe I was motivated by fear of the unknown and-- Well, no similarity or parallel to something makes something else reasonable. The fact I was mostly not afraid to experience the unknown cannot provide a reason. Weak induction is usually dangerous. With weak induction, the mystery is lost and the poetry dies. It is therefore better for me to stop this and go back to looking outside. It is still snowing and I do not dare listen to another song.

II

We always fall in love in the language of the country most recently victorious. In the language of the victorious, we write elegies for the defeated who have not yet been buried. I don't know why I can't sleep at night. Last year, I worked in a restaurant at night, cleaning the toilets.

Everybody left and my job started. One toilet stall was locked from the inside. With a spare key, I unlocked the stall and opened it. A drunk girl was sleeping there. I woke her up and brought her coffee. In an unknown language, she talked and cried. She was drunk and unable to understand the language of the victorious. I don't know why, instead of the warmth of her skin or the sorrow in her eyes or the thirst of her crying, I thought about the bombardment. Who am I to consider her characteristics? Was I measuring her with myself or independently? Her body that night was without a history. So why did I have to read her into my history? Could I have wanted to conquer her or let her conquer me? Anyway, her body cannot be the subject for negotiating about the bombardment. What if, when she was drinking her coffee, I was sitting closer to her? What if I was crying too? It was dawn when both of us left by the same door. I did not dare to touch her. Her body was alive. I don't know whether this fear came from the unknown or death. Perhaps both. But every midnight, next to the door of my toilet, my heart beat faster and there was nobody in there.

III

Your body is a bird. My love is a dead bird. What is similar about the body and the bird? Do I want to relate two fears? Which is more important-- recognizing their similarity or understanding each of them? Why do I insist on seeing the two fears as equivalent to each other? Why do I borrow your body to make this comparison? Who benefits from this metaphor? A living bird does not cry for a dead bird. But why now, when it is dawn, do I occupy myself with this duality? Perhaps because nobody signed the order to bombard during the day? But many are being killed on the stairs or in the toilet. This song cries for something. Maybe for this reason, I fell in love in it. I don't know. You haven't heard this song. I can not know the bird's opinion. But I understand the crying of my body. In this song, in this place on the paper, passengers are going to their offices and a girl is facing the window and drinking her last coffee. I, in the hour of ghosts, jumped out of your sleep. My body is a dead bird.

I tie my horse to the handle of the door.
I strew papers from the saddle bags on the floor .
I take you on a tour of the ruins,
the ruins of stories.
I kiss you
on the hand of the hero of that story,
on the leg of the anti-hero of another story,
on shoes, clothes, songs.
You are not smiling in the rhythm of goodbyes.
I do not cry with the music of *hello*s.
Whenever I say hello to a woman
I just salute her.
And whenever I say goodbye
I say it to all women.
On the ruins of the stories
the *hello* is temporary,
the kiss is temporary,
the ruins are eternal.
My horse is somewhere in the ruins.
No one comes,
no one goes.

I wanted to be a physicist.
Your kisses made me a poet.
Before that
I built two wireless devices.
I knew the speed
of the waves
of your voice,
how they were multiplied
in my earphones;
and at which distances
one could hear
instances
of your voice.
I was supposed to discover a formula
to gather
the scattered energy of you
from space,
to recreate your body
with smiles and tears.
In your embrace,
I was measuring
the friction
factor:
skin on skin,
fluid on fluid.
The coefficient
of gravity,
the exact location of
landing
in centrifugal
motion.

I didn't know
how to calculate
the frequency of your kisses,
which aspect
to divide,
with what distance between us.
In your embrace,
every time,
I was catapulted to the stars
at the speed of light
and each time
you became younger.
Now
with all my knowledge
of physics,
I can only measure
the mass of a black hole
transforming
every living body
into the energy
of silence.

He said:
The target is
our false enemy,
and the moon smiled.
It was also possible
they didn't start a fire.
It was also possible
they didn't yell.
It was also possible
the moon didn't smile.
Now even if it were Armstrong
himself,
even if it were Hiroshima,
even if it were the siren
of an ambulance
or a police car,
surely it was possible
to find a way
for the moon
not to shine
through a window
on the third floor.
They were forced
to hospitalize her.
And tomorrow,
when her photos are
front page news,
she will become
a political prisoner.

The Abysmal

I

The stairs of 2 o'clock are eternalized at 2 o'clock,
the streets of 3 at 3 o'clock,
the metal tea cup and the junk chair at 4 o'clock.
I'm afraid of the eternity of objects.
Nobody receives my memory from me.
This is our last meeting, or I never met you.
You bring your lips close, or move them back.
Your scarf is green, or violet.
You distance yourself from objects
and the objects turn eternal in me.

I sit on the same stairs even if I'm in another city.
I drink from the same tea cup even if it's a coffee cup.
I wheel myself around on the same chair,
in the car, in my bed, in the plane.
Objects stick to the hands of the clock.
I am addicted to my eternity.

II

Memory is more painful than history.
Genghis Khan
is making a minaret out of heads.
I don't know the smell of their hair.
Page by page cities are being ruined
and no walls fall on me.
From the memory of my father
no perfume stops me in the street.

I read one line with a fallen head,
I blink,
I reach the next fallen head.
Genghis Khan attacks the history of your hands,
hands with chewed off fingernails,
the disappearing trace of a ring,
the cut of broken glass or a kitchen knife.

I kiss your fingertips.
I bury the cut heads.

III

Take away from me the street that hurts,
the window that hurts,
the red curtains,
the red sofas,
the perfume that stops me in the street,
all colors,
my habit of kissing,
the heat of my body making love,
my excitement in the dark stairs of your home,
so I can become a book
of history that suffers less,
so the distance between Genghis Khan and Halaku
can be just a few pages.

IV

I am all the battles I have not fought in
all the women I did not love,
all the notes I didn't hum to you,

all your untold stories.
The eternity of objects
multiplies you in all the absences.
It robs me of the memory of my mother,
my red bed, the linen tiger of your son,
your pink skirt.
I don't know if I am the silk road or a black hole in space.
Merchants pass through me.
They discount your smile in the bazaars.
The voice of street hawkers
is wandering in the galaxy.
I pass my memory with the speed of light.
Lightning is bitter,
the mine field is bitter,
the Qajar coffee is bitter.
The wine in my skull,
hemlock,
the speed of light—all are bitter.
I wander through space
and my black purity is heavy.

The moon always shines in vain
and wars don't start without reason,
but the one who goes and the one who remains
are both defeated by accident.
So look into my eyes
as you pack your bags
and say your goodbyes.
Without regret
you will carry the joy of your last cigarette
until the train starts to leave,
because truth is the child of regret
and I don't want to be your truth.
So close your eyes
and kiss me
until the metal of your kisses melts in my veins
and gets cast in the indifference of the moon,
because the train is approaching the station,
that is to say—beauty is the child of impossibility,
and gets to be possible only in the womb of despair,
where my skin
is the imagination of the earth
at the moment you
crush your cigarette with your foot
and you turn eternal.

Searchlights halt
on the sculpture of the full moon
in the abandoned station
at the moment of bombardment.

I respect scales.
They can assign numbers to anything.
They can balance anything.
Me and the apple,
the apple and you,
you and me.

I stand on the scale.
I call the sunset and the mist.
I wave to the lighted lamps,
I make present in myself the street and the rain,
all the hurrying passersby,
you and your smile,
you and your tears.
The scale does not move,
It does not pay attention.

I respect the scale.

You give me happiness
like the city that each night
gives me unnumbered luminous lamps.

You take off your clothes,
the city is stuck to your skin.
It's sunset.

Rush hour—everybody goes home
to turn on their lamps
and my embrace and my kisses
are stuck in traffic.

Slowly, slowly, I close the curtains.
I turn off the lamps one by one,
and all the elevators
keep
going down.

Laws of Gravity

I

On your planet, an apple falls from the tree
and Newton discovers the laws of gravity.

On my planet, the telephone rings.
Newton picks up the receiver,
is hurled into the air,
and gets stuck in the branches of a tree.
I prefer to sit
on the principles of natural philosophy
and bite
floating apples—
which is to say,
I want to weep a little.

II

A street where no dog barks
is a dead street.
The dogs with lolling tongues
pant
and grab the pants of a passing poet.
The poet takes off his pants
and his shirt
and naked as the day he was born
escapes into the world.
The dogs bark
and run from one street to another.
A poet who forgets all his words doesn't have any weight,

he turns into a straw in the wind.
The wind howls in the howling of the wolves.
The wolves escape in the snow,
which is burying the streets.

Your history
makes my eternity less.

An untold capacity is scattered in the air.
It makes the sidewalks narrow,
it changes the names of alleys.
My eternity stands, waiting for a date,
asking all the passersby what time it is.

In the distance between restlessness and doubt,
the mountain snows melt.
Water drowns the street.
Some walk underwater.
Some sit on floating boards.
On one board, a man plays a violin.
Underwater, a woman plays a piano.

The violin is on fire.
Its voice flies away from the fire
and goes to the water.
The piano rots.
Its voice climbs to the surface of the water.
The man takes the voice of the piano in his burned hands.
The woman catches the voice of the violin in her decayed hands.
The voices stare into eyes.
They are begging.
The woman is floating on the water.
The man is floating on the water.
The voice of your steps comes from the depths of the water.
The street is mute.
It disappears.

My eternity
sits in a cafe,
pours you tea,
takes your hand.
Your history
turns the tea stormy.
The doors of the coffee shop slam shut.
Your hands hide under the table.
Your caresses escape from me.
Your voice flees.
An untold capacity
is sitting at the next table.
I am floating on the water.
You are gone.

—Didn't I leave my hat in your voice, lady?
—Yes, but the wind took it away!
—What about my shoes?
—They are there—two sparrows are nesting in them.

I run.
I get naked.

The lava of your voice enfolds me.
I don't have time to breathe.
I turn to stone
on the threshold of crescendo and diminuendo.
Centuries later
a photo of me will be published:
standing in the remains of Pompeii's eruption,
barefoot,
hatless.

You looked at me
and a far-away window opened and closed.
You stroked me
and I got wet
from the rain beyond that window.
You are here beside me
and with your every movement
something moves in the distance,
which makes something move in me.
I was born in the year of your exile.
In your eyes a woman was making dolls.
In the shape of all her dead she was making dolls
and was setting them
on the window sill in front of my eyes.
One had my hat on his head.
Another was wearing my shoes.
I was being created from her losses.

You were looking at me
and the rain was still raining
on your suitcases
and the shoes and the hats of the dead.
I kiss you
and we exchange
losses.

Newton's Elegies

Stones were blocking the river's way.
I was carrying fish in my hands,
in the restlessness of bodies,
in the turbulence of a pail going up the valley
to the pool inhabited by the hungry look of cats.
The stones were your eyes,
the fish, the words of my sonnets
that in the year of the earthquake
were joined to the four elements.
Newton's hair was covered with pebbles,
Newton's hair was smeared with mercury,
the vapor of mercury was poisoning the paper,
it was killing kings.

Newton was the acceleration of fish in
the restlessness of the pail
in which he wanted to take stones from the river,
and the earth was heavy,
and his words became fish,
his hair turned to poison.
Sad eyes,
joking eyes
covered by moss,
next to each other on each other
form the walls of a prison
where Newton's Second Law is being tortured.
I was exiled to the First Law
where neither the sound of breathing on the telephone
nor the calm growth of moss under contact lenses
could reach—

just Newton's solidifying voice
and the clots of blood on the surface of the prison
wrote me.
Mercury is the struggle of eternity,
stone is the age of earth in Newton's Second Law,
the law condemned by the relativity of your eyes
that is released from Dachau
and scatters in the galaxy along with the Berlin Wall.
Sad eyes,
joking eyes,
hang from Newton's hair,
in my abyss,
the language.
With the first kiss
language attains
universal dimensions:
kisses build a temple
on Newton's Third Law
which later
falls on Hiroshima.
The lips of cold wars,
the lips of geography...
Mercury trembles in the mirror.
A pail of water
has been thrown on my image.
The fish
are stuck to the magnet of my body.
The meat-eating fish,
the small fish of the pool,
are swimming within my borders.
Their eyes are stones in the mirrors,
the eyelids of the void,

the eyelids of oblivion.
O, solitude of Newton on the lips of women,
o, vapor of mercury in the lullabies of mothers,
o, philosopher's stone and tear gas.
Night sits back against the salt licks.
The moon shakes off the footsteps of astronauts,
and your eyes overflow with time.
Your tears pass
from Newton's nightmares
into my poems,
the words in a river of tears
hatch.

O, the cold shroud of the paper,
o, the white eternity,
o, the absolute snow.

My skull's
a cup of wine
and a Chinese painter
painted
on the edge
a herd
of
horses
racing
inebriated.
Inside
my
head
they whinny.
The cup falls,
images
escape,
as well as
the horses.

From every loss a phantasm is born:
the daughter that I never had
is crying on the rooftop.
The poem I never wrote
became the paper's nightmare.
The daughter I never had
reads the poem I never wrote
and it's raining on the rooftop
and the rain washed the paper and took it away.
The paper turned into the subject of loss,
like my skin,
which is lost to me
when your hands
are not here.

Because of their functions, objects will not be repeated.
The lighter burns.
The pen writes.
Your memory
occupies objects.
Every resistance
must transform the functions of objects.
It should be possible to write with the lighter
and light a cigarette with the pen,
or one could go even farther,
to where objects
reject being in our history,
like your eyes
reject looking at me
on this snowy night
when snow burns
and the fire is cold.

Each time the man arrived at the dreams of the woman
something disappeared from around him:
by stopping the conversation
the window was turning invisible.
The return of objects was impossible
unless the man followed a reverse path
all the way to the moment
when distance turned to mass
and time to space.
Around the man
everything became invisible
except himself.
He tried to imagine all the lost objects
and, for example, to steal the wall from
the woman's hands,
but in everything
he found the objectness of another object:
in the wall, the window,
in the window, the trees,
in the trees, the paper,
in the paper, himself.
He realized that he'd been dead for a long time.
Dream by dream,
the woman
was erasing his memories
of the objects:
she was in love with someone else.

The history of colonialism
does not let me dock in you.
I myself, like Colombus,
had the intention of India
and your shore was unexpected.
I didn't know that the earth is round,
and the color of a shirt in childhood
in a flat city
one day will take me to a body
that from east to west,
from north to south,
is full of unknown languages,
and my words are not in their vocabulary.

I am no explorer, no victor.
I didn't know that the earth is round
and time is circular,
and for a kiss
I have to turn back history
to the time before I sailed
from your skirt,
and there is only wind
and the dark violet of your shirt
in a street that has no name yet
for a kid that hasn't started speaking.

Death is when the heart does not beat and the clock beats.
Love is when the heart beats and the clock does not beat.
Perhaps this simple comparison explains
why you glanced at your watch.
You knew that waiting is the dense endurance of eternity,
and love, the miracle of mortals,
makes eternity ashamed,
but death does not wait for anybody.

The long summer afternoon
was going down on coffins and clock towers.
The ruins knew,
and you did not know,
that war makes waiting invalid
and saving life
the whole Truth.

Was she dead?
Had she fled without you?
Or were you not in love any more?
The dead were not answering.
The living were escaping.
And love from then on
beat within
the pulsing of a clock.

We Were Always Traveling

I

We were always traveling,
and the place was one of three types:

the one that was becoming memory,
the one that was escaping from sight,
the one which fit in a suitcase.

Time interferes with memory.
The heart of dreams beats in a place that escaped.
The suitcase closes
and opens,
and one place mixes with another.

The destination
was not the dream
or the memory,
but a suitcase
on its way to the cemetery.

Sunset on graves and
the smell of summer on the grass.

You decompose
in the image of totality,
having escaped from sight
you are always in sight.

II

With closed eyes
I look at your eyes—
when I open my eyes
the wind
turns
the empty pages.

On the other side of the street
a pink dress,
soft nakedness:

this side,
the young smell of death
in white sheets:

poetry
is not the funeral procession,
is not the epiphany behind the curtain,
it is the curtain
drawn over
both.

The first was a woman I loved,
then a woman who loved me,
then a woman not able to sleep,
then a woman from whose hands something was always
falling.
After that a woman who took a knife
and stabbed it into the bellies of her dolls,
after that a woman who escaped from the house.
I haven't been with any other woman.

With how many men
are you coming to my bed?

Losses,
not in our nature
but in our human intention,
happen.

However the body enjoys
kissing you or her,

the invention of the human being
might have been a mistake.

Snow falls without reason
and the poem written with a human intention
does not heal.

Kiss me!

Today
all the turns I took
were wrong
and each time
I had to go all the way back.

Days do not have any other destination,
but this poem
and I
always
come too late.

I told her: give me a word,
I will give you a poem!
She told me: bring your lips closer,
I will give birth to a word.
I was afraid
and ran away from the day of resurrection.
For years
in this poem
I've been waiting for death.

Each farewell
takes part of the deep
with it.
Laughter
in a struggle to go that far
reaches the frontiers of the void,
floating
without gravity.
The galaxy of farewell
does not have
any sun.

Returning from a trip:
left over from the last party
is a rotten apple.
I throw it away.

Shame
or forgetfulness
are not abstractions.
A kiss which was withdrawn
that summer morning
took you to another city.

Returning from all trips
I clean the table
and nothing is left.

The Narration of History within the Calendar of Betrayal

*To Neda Agha-Soltan**

I was protesting in silence,
in the labyrinth of your body,
on your bruised streets,
in the footprints of the garbage men,
who every morning washed away wounds and kisses
so that I would always see myself as alone.
My nightmares expire on your body,
but in poetry nothing has an expiration date.
Poetry stands face to face with the word,
with a handkerchief tied around its face.
Not tear gas,
nor the new Chinese armored cars
could stop the stones from landing in Tiananmen Square.
Poetry stands face to face with the word
in order to be as closely in contact with your body as possible,
though the guard's uniform fits you.
You can send one hundred word-garrisons out into the street,
still poetry lives in the silence between words,
in the chaotic distance between *smile* and *you*,
in the violent trembling of your body the moment before
the touch of my hands
that don't capture you
but strip you naked of
the camera, the megaphone, and the news,
the courier, the town crier, and the news,
the word, and the news.

---

* **Neda Agha Soltan** was killed in 2009 on Amir-Abad Street in Tehran; she died at about 5 PM.

Everything is luminous:
the falling rain,
the creek,
the red apple that floats away.
A word sits on your tongue
and black imagination runs through the streets.
The blood
is dark in your veins.
The ashes of Hallaj
are sprinkled on the Tigris of your body
and a black flood
swallows the wandering red apples.
Smile!
Let me dip my shirt in the Tigris
so that perhaps my new man's odor
can save the city.

Olympus was dark.
All the numbers,
all the letters were dark.
Black snow was falling.
The storks were not returning home.
And your hesitant fingers
were stumbling over the dark letters.
Invisible waves
made wounded deer appear on my shirt.
Your voice was in Hell
and Hell was inside the belly of a snake.
I bit the wandering apples
in order to make the snake give birth
and the sin of your voice
called forth colors—

and red flowers,
and the fire.
In heaven I knew only the names.
The elevator was coming up
and I was falling into verbs.
You passed through the doorway
and suffixes stuck to objects,
verbs were being conjugated in the first-person singular,
the second-person plural,
in the past and future tense.
The elevator was coming up
and the axis of the earth tilted.
I was at the equator,
I was at the pole,
with you.

The elevator was going down
and I, in the silence between words,
heard the homeless sounds,
the shaking of Shibli's hand touching the redness of the rose,
the weeping of the air at the moment he threw the rose,
and the silent outcry of Hallaj at the moment he was hit by the rose,
or the howling of the third-person singular at the moment
you surrendered
the heat of your kisses.
Couldn't you have refrained from saying, *I'm okay, everything is fine,*
and refrained from digging more mass graves?
Couldn't you have talked about the burnt piano and
the voice of helicopters
so at least you wouldn't have denied the Holocaust?

When the poem steps into the street, all the adjectives
disappear.
It's blocked ahead.
You have to walk backwards down blurred, narrow alleys
and you've forgotten where the crosswalks are.
Hurriedly, you dip your fingers in the jar of ink,
covering up "we resist"
on the walls you used to be able to lean against,
and now, in the rushed pressure of your hands, they
collapse.
No dust rises.
The houses are empty.
The antique burnt piano is left in the alley,
mute, it doesn't respond to the gesture of your hands ,
under your fingers, it turns to powder
and its mute notes
scatter in your black and white sunset.
[black]
[white]
Your red boots
flee in the silence of the alley.

In the distance between word and object
spiders are weaving a web.
The webs of epochs have covered your mouth.
The corpses of wandering pronouns drop in my mouth
when I kiss you.
I kiss you and my melted words
become shoes you wear,
a new perfume you put on.
Every night I dream of corpses
falling from your mouth into my abyss,

wandering sounds that have no resurrection
in exile.

Exile is a barrel of acid.
When your army approaches the city
the moon sinks in the well
and I decompose to language.
Language decomposes to words
and words decompose to sounds
that cannot travel along telephone lines.
I decompose on the webs of your mouth
and the moon
rises from the throat of a woman
I have never kissed.

The wind was coming. It was howling.
I didn't want to meet her in the picture frame.
I didn't want to browse through the pages of the photo album
to see eyes that could not smile.
Windows were slamming into one another.
I didn't know how many streets I was away from her.
I saw her in the dusk of anecdotes,
in the browsing of photo albums.
With a gun and a cartridge belt she
was twirling a red flower in her hand,
page after page,
she was inserting petals,
page after page.
The wind was slamming doors.
I was gathering petals from the pages.
I was lying down naked,
raining petals on myself.

The wind was blowing, it was howling .
They made a circle around her,
amazed by the moon
that, red,
was rising from her throat
on Amir-Abad Street
at five in the afternoon.
No! I don't want to see her.
Let the moon come.
Dust was covering her moonlit face,
covering the photo albums.

There were many of them.
They were coming back from their silent protest,
from exile,
and all night long the wind
covered the city with petals.

Meaning is utopian.
Utopia is a mother
dead in my infancy:
unreachable,
like meaning,
like writing this midnight,
when the voices of childhood come back
and childhood does not.

Capitalism
or socialism?
When the ideal of one man
is the reality of another,
the cruelty of life
is not only
in the paradox of divine justice,
chance,
and your beauty.
Just because
you do not love him any more
you would not love me later on,
even if you were mine,
thus universal pain continues.
Perhaps your freedom,
his possession,
and my ideals
are the creators of this continuous pain.
Certainly death is kinder,
because desire
leads us to betrayal
or poetry,
which, like this snow,
falls unstoppably
on our hidden bed
and is crueler
than any human being.

In foreign languages
I have just one name:
the name my mother gave me.
In my mother tongue,
a thousand foreign names.

A father that does not kill his son
sooner or later
will commit suicide.

The legacy of the wind:
an abandoned house,
broken windows.

Yesterday while awake
I saw my death in a dream.
I was ten years younger.
In a scene where my mother
was crying over my body,
I started crying,
as if the one who was dreaming
and the one who had died
were two persons.

Suddenly I understood your current regret:
the one who left me ten years ago
and the one who was crying today
were two persons.
Yes, both of us
had entered the dream of a house
abandoned
since the death of my mother.

Don’t tell me I’m not that kind of person!
I get to be possible only in my death.
Now I am someone
who rejects himself.
Those unimportant details
will disappear in death:
this habit of leaving the window half open at bedtime,
or the fear of the whiteness of snow,
or my obsession with the type of paper.
After my death
you will close the window.
Outside the window it is snowing.
You will write me the way you like,
without superstition,
without fear.

A ruined land
is not
a wasteland,
an abandoned house,
or an empty bed.

It's the ruin, the one who ruins, and the act of ruining.
Its geography is cruelty.
Point by point
its map has been marked by everything it lacks:

it is a hand throwing a stone at the window,
it is the window breaking,
it is a piece of glass wounding my hand.
A ruined land
is not blood.
It is the invader:

it is you
who measure
my capability
not by my kisses
but by how much you own.

Sleepless dawn:
I open the window:
the unclear voice of a child.

From the window
no child is visible.

As it is every morning,
this pillow is wet.
The sleep you haven't slept
fills your awakening.

So unreachable am I
that only love or death
can take me out of my orbit.
I revolve around a word
that empties other words.
My four seasons
are all one season:
exile.

A tree grows in that season
in the shape of a tree,
with the functions of a tree,
even its shadow
is like the shadow of a tree,
but it is not a tree.

Today I am violently trembling.
A bird lands on the branch,
which immediately
is a bird.
Death or love?
I don't know.
One of them is close.

The Poem

for Reza Allameh-Zadeh

I

Words are the burial ground of things.
The sound of the horse galloping in these lines
is a sound I haven't heard since childhood.
And your laughter decayed in my adolescence.
I write
as if on a pilgrimage to the city of the dead.
If by chance time travels backward,
the murmurs of my father
resound in the ear of the text, and the voice of a bullet
disturbs the dream of the lines,
and the poem with mussed up hair
walks around a room decaying for years.
Words are scattered on the faded blueprint of a house.
Here is the window.
Outside the window is the courtyard. Nobody knows
which nightmare awakens a poem.
Sometimes the window and the secret glance of a neighbor's
bride.
Sometimes the swing and the bicycle,
or the wall with all its cheap paintings.
It looks at them hard in order to become alive
and in the space between the inhalation and the
exhalation
of living things
it goes back to sleep.

II

Years ago, the murmurs of my father
got lost in the dream of a text
and the poem lit three thousand candles,
made three thousand paper boats,
and gave them all to the ocean.
Now that I've packed my bags
and am waiting for the first train
that won't bring me back,
the poem is riding a bicycle.
Trembling, rushing headlong,
it pedals over potholes and through puddles,
rings a doorbell, stares at whispers
and moans, afraid of being heard.
In the ear of the text, the whispers are so loud
that it's impossible to hear the whistle of a train.
I am still in the station
and the poem in Khavaran
pushes people who've been dead for years
out of eyesight of the guards.

III

A year ago
the poem slipped through a gap in barbed wire
where the soldiers stood guard on the hills of your breasts.
It stole your lips
and it stole your hands,
in order to recreate your body.
This year, the soldiers stand guard on the edge of nothingness:
your body has been stolen.

In the station,
a dead person is in my seat,
whose name the poem doesn't know.
(It can't learn your name, either.)
The bullet and warm blood
sink into the lines.
No paper can stop the bleeding.
The station is full of travelers, all dead.
The firing squads
and hanging ropes
aren't waiting for a train.
The murmur of the gravediggers
rings the doorbell of three thousand houses.
Three thousand bicycles are abandoned
in the alleys.

IV

No poem ever stood in front of a firing squad.
And the firing squad
does not know at which part of the poem it must aim.
It just increases the price of water and electricity,
rent, and the cost of being buried.
I cannot buy cigarettes for three thousand dead,
but I can make them all alive.
I don't want to force the poem
to return them to a cemetery
that no longer exists.
I just want to remind the poem
that nobody will listen to the repeated ringing of the doorbell,
and all the abandoned bicycles have decayed.
They will stay at the station.

And if the poem can take a ticket from each reader,
it will put them on the first one-way train.
In my homeland,
three thousand dead in a station is natural,
three thousand dead on a train is natural.

V

At checkpoint stations,
they detain our language.
Our words decay when passing that border.
I let go of your hands outside the station,
the whistle of the train flusters my words.
Words occupy all the compartments.
They have thousand-year-old nightmares.
My words are young,
just thirty years old.
But under these prison clothes,
layer upon layer,
they keep accumulating.
Yellow is not the color of my first school shoes.
Red, not the color of my piggy bank,
blue, not the color of my first bicycle.
The words ripened with the colors of your skirt.
They were a herd of weeping horses,
a rainbow you were taking off
to send arcing through the air,
falling into mud
and handcuffs, darkness, and the command, *Fire!*

VI

I'm not standing in this long line for bread and milk.
I'm standing here to turn over my language.
Everything gets lighter when it crosses the border.
I'm standing here to be translated.
A bicycle patrols my borders,
pedaling over potholes and through puddles.
The poem gazes at conjunctions and prepositions,
in the distance between I and I,
I to from on I.
It's raining
on conjunctions and prepositions,
on relations.
In the rain,
I distance myself from you.
And Khavaran, in the distance between me and you,
expands.

VII

In my language
every time everybody suddenly falls silent,
a policeman is born.
In my language
on the back of each frightened bicycle,
three thousand dead words are sitting.
In my language,
in murmurs, they make confessions,
in whispers, they wear black,
in silence,
they get buried.

My language is silence.

Who will translate my silence?

How can I cross this border?

It's land and water that write these lines.
It's memory and oblivion that write these lines.
The whiteness of the paper finds itself in your hands
and the empty paper, the unread poem,
is moistened with your tears.
The tears turn to vapor in the caress of my hands.
From the darkness of the primeval sea
a hard wind is enfolded in my shirt
and shakes the bones,
and wet words fall on the paper
from cracks in my skin.
It's land and water.
It's memory and oblivion,
and the share of oblivion in the body
is always more than memory.
Without it, it's impossible to swim in any sea,
it's impossible to embrace anybody's body.
And the salt of the sea is the word,
and the skeleton of the dead is the word.
When I dig the tomb of my body
I dig your tomb in an unreachable land,
and the wind, the essence of dreams,
from the far-off primeval sea,
is enfolded in my shirt.
On the shore of the paper,
water dances
around your feet:
again white
and delicate.

I'm going to swim.

An image
initiates the voyage
and the voyage passes through kisses,
wars,
thirst, and intoxication.

Your image
is the totality of my voyage,
without being my destination.

In the distance between your image and you
time is sitting
and will never leave either one of us.

One day in the doorway
with a kiss
we will be added to the absences within your image.

In the white window behind me
the curtain is open
and a little girl on a blue bicycle
crosses the street.
Old men are drinking their morning coffee.
It's a cold day.
The sea is roaring.

There are two types of readers:
those who pay attention to the appearance of the wound,
those who pay attention to its consequences:
appearance and essence—
death
that reads and is being read.
Autumn visits all the houses.
From the open window
the wind
brings a dry leaf into the room.
I do not want any reader.
Close the window.
Come closer.
O, you, unfaithful one,
o, you, the poem.

Lost Fragments

I

I blacked out all the words in that lined notebook
to veil your face
and the wind
carried along the feathers of birds
and life
was full of fugitive words.
The paper fluttered a moment on the barbed wire
and the text overflowed with the neighing of the circling
horse covered with lashes from a cloud whiter than paper.
The sun was shining,
the alley was moist.

Take me back to the same place,
so I can black out that word—
how hard this rain is raining...

Gone—not gone.
The alley whistles a toe-tapping song
and your footsteps stop in mid-air,
where my words are flapping their wings.

II

I leave you in that first fragment
to calm my horse
on this bump in the road made by whispers of
the winds of glances,
and the falling rain named the second fragment,

and the stork trembled, having lost her way,
and the day starts with the game of glances.
I am a fragment of this incomplete fragment.
Try not to slip on the neighs.
And the blacked out saddlebag got the stork with child.

Take me back to the same place,
so I can leave that word untold—
this rain does not stop falling...

Fled—not fled.
A pinwheel spins in the alley's hand
and a smile gets printed
on the wall
where you're writing graffiti.

III

The king left!
I myself heard it in this fragment
and the sea was appalled by
your management of the anchor
and the ship remained heavier than the cloud you were painting.
The king forgot he was gone
and nailed me like a proclamation to the wall.
The street cleaners touched your family tree
and I turned to water in the songs of poor sailors
and anchored the ship wherever you left footprints
and I wrote footnotes to the days:

Take me back to the same place,
so I don't see the same word—
how hard this rain is lashing!

Said—not said.
The comet rolls nearer
and the thread breaks in the alley's hands
and you are appalled
by the paper that in this fragment
loses its life.

IV

I don't know why the ship anchors in this fragment
and the slaves disembark and stand on the drums
and the alley shakes itself free of suffering
to keep away the genie that wears your clothes.
With my hands in my pockets I whistled by
and crossed out my name from this fragment
and the passersby were running inside the text
and I left the margin of the paper
and I was searching for you
to crumple my new poem
and the train whistle runs on the lines.

Take me back to the same place,
so I can kill the same word—
how unexpected is this falling rain!

Tired—not tired.
The kid makes a paper rocket
and the alley explodes on passersby
and the leaves of wind
are turned
by your hands.

V

The fire increases in this fragment
and you warm up your hands by the fire
and the wind spurs the neighs
and the stork
flies out of the crosshatches of my shirt
and with the next whistle of the train
the passengers will disembark
and my eyes go snow-blind in the blankness of the paper
and the alley in this poem is always moist
and the genie sleeps in this fragment:

Take me back to the same place,
where I do not live for the same word—
since this rain falls without question...

Exist—not exist.
The alley plays hopscotch with the girl
who loses her life in one of the squares
and your tears
cut the heads off words
in the doorway of a fragment
that has not yet arrived.

VI

Everything arrives in an unarrived fragment
and that fragment is unalterably
shackled to the feet of the poem
so the poet will learn not to say anything more about that alley
and let the train run off the line

and discharge its passengers on the roofs of the houses.
Everything comes from a fragment still unarrived
and such a fragment can
be asleep on the backs of horses
or in your eyes.

No! Bring me back to the same place,
so I don't return to this place—
how unutterably the rain is falling

Arrived—not arrived.
Words jam together
and your eyes
can never be expressed.

I wrote a poem: full of waiting and rain,
a poem where all my hair turned white,
a poem that tapped its beak on the window
and the window remained closed.
But the walls are scraped away,
and the doors are slammed shut,
and the soldiers are still in my hands.

I wrote a poem full of waiting and rain,
and there, instead of the lines of the paper,
snakes were slithering.
I go to write your name
and the snakes wrap around my hand
and pull me inside,
to the depth of the whiteness of the paper.
I call you.
And when the tears make the paper wet,
the words wake up from a heavy sleep,
they yawn, shave, they put on their uniforms and start to march.
But a word standing in front of the mirror
combs her hair,
smiles,
opens the door,
and leaves.
The rain keeps raining.
She will be wet. Certainly—she will catch cold.

I wake up.
My poem has been removed
and I have an umbrella.

Yamsa: A Tribute to Absence

In memory of Farzad Kamangar

I

I'm sitting at the end of the world
in Yamsa,
on a small island
you can walk around
in an hour—
sufficient time for you to know
the date you are waiting for
is not coming.
Fifty years ago, it was bought.
They built some wooden cottages,
a fireplace and an oven,
and I arrived there by boat.
It is rainy
at the end of the world.
Swans and boats are floating on the water.
Death does not come here.
I was sitting on the boat
when she, with her green eyes,
was speaking to me about the age of soldier's boots,
which, in her land, last for more than fifty years,
the fact that she misses me,
and loves fire,
and blue flames.
The end of the world will not come again.

---

* **Farzad Kamangar** was a 32-year-old teacher, poet, journalist, human rights activist and social worker who was hanged on May 9, 2010. At his execution, he offered chocolates to all the observers.

Always, there is only one end
and nobody can interpret it.

II

In Yamsa
nobody speaks his own language.
In winter when the lakes are frozen
wolves and humans come here walking.
This place was never uninhabited.
Everything that came here came in its perfection,
your beauty, my impossibility,
and in its intensity
language always disappears.
One can only point to objects.
People come to Yamsa with abstract nouns,
but in the first fire
abstractions and wood burn together
and the taste of chocolate
turns to ash in the mouth.
When the chair is pushed out from under the feet of
a hanging man and
absurdity and meaning
both refer to the chocolate wrapper
at the same time the stage is emptied
of the killer and the killed, the viewer and the viewed,
and the cleaner sweeps up the chocolate remains.
Sitting at the end of the world,
the wind crawls into the fire and all the flames are blue.

III

Absence is when you can point out
all of someone's attributes—
her green eyes,
her moonlight skin and her lips which are
red—
but you cannot point at her.
Or when the woman who lies beside you
does not have a nightmare
that makes your hands's caress a necessity.
This is the reason God is always absent,
whether the chair is pushed out from under my feet
or I sit in Yamsa on a chair
and the *you* of my poems changes.
In all the world wars
no bomb ever fell at the end of the world.
It has never been occupied,
no savior ever fit there.
At the end of the world
I am burning papers
where the skin of women and my hands
mingle with decorations.
Boats row in nothingness,
the wind crawls into empty houses,
and all the flames are blue.

IV

In Yamsa
time transubstantiates into experience.
A day is the distance in feet between newly-arrived boats

and never-arriving boats.
A year is the distance
measured in hands
it takes my hands to reach your hair.
And eternity is taller than the height of a human,
the height of a pushed-away chair.
When the feet no longer move
and the doctor-in-charge determines
the rope can be taken away,
the rope is taken away,
and I get empty in the transubstantiation of boat into boat,
hand into hair,
and body into memory.
I transmute to a place in Yamsa,
a grave, a cradle
where blue flames
are the only burning metaphor that flickers,
just like a date
at the end of the world.

V

I'm sitting here
in Yamsa
in shadow and reflection,
song and the river,
tears and the breath of infinity,
in a boat which brings me back
to you and my Palestine,
to me and your Kurdistan.
Arsenic burns blue,
lead burns green.

Arsenic and lead,
poison and bullet,
burn in us.
We miss each other,
and both are indebted to absence.

It is rainy.
The trains are delayed.
At the last station,
with a blue umbrella,
I'm searching for a woman
with a red umbrella
and green eyes.

With every *I wish* we construct a paradise,
I wish I were kissing her!

In this paradise
the wind dishevels her hair,
her cheeks are streaked with tears,
Troy is burning.
Ghosts weigh us in the scale of her eyes.

I wish I weren't kissing her!
Shivering,
we climb the stairs of hell.

The wind dishevels her hair even more.
She wipes away her tears and smiles.
The ghosts escape.
We are standing on earth,
imagining another paradise.

INDEX

Mohsen Emadi (Iran, 1976) is a poet, translator, and filmmaker. He has published four books of poetry in Spain and Iran. He has translated Vladimir Holan, Nichita Stanescu, Jiri Orten, Antonio Gamoneda, Juan Gelman, Cesar Vallejo, Alejandra Pizarnik, Luis Cernuda, José Gorostiza, Clara Janés, Walt Whitman, Milan Rufus, and others. In 2007 he founded the online *Persian Anthology of World Poetry,* which he continues to edit. His poetry has been translated into Arabic, Bangla, Bulgarian, Catalan, French, Japanese, Portuguese, Slovakian, and Spanish. He has screened his documentaries *Dear Antonio,* about the poetry of Antonio Gamoneda, and *A Poet and His Exile,* about Luis Cernuda's exile in Mexico, in Mexico, Portugal, and Spain. After the contested election of 2009, he left Iran as a political exile. After living in several European countries, he settled in Mexico, where he splits his time between Mexico City, where he is doing doctoral research about digital poetry at UNAM, and Malincalo, where he collaborates on several cultural projects for the University of Mexico State. His poetic work has been recognized with the 2010 Premio Poesía de Miedo, a Finnish Literature Exchange Fellowship, the IV Antonio Machado Fellowship, an ICORN Fellowship, and the 2015 "Poets from Other Worlds" honor from the International Poetry Fund.

Lyn Coffin is a widely published poet, translator, playwright, and fiction writer. Her translation of Rustaveli's *The Knight in the Panther Skin* appeared in 2015. She has published nineteen books. She teaches professional and continuing education at the University of Washington and lives in Seattle.

www.ingramcontent.com/pod-product-compliance
Lightning Source LLC
Jackson TN
JSHW081409170426
101040JS00015B/336

* 9 7 8 1 9 4 4 7 0 0 0 0 3 *